Waltham Fore

THIS WALKER BOOK BELONGS TO:

_____

_____

_____

For Araminta and Rufus

First published 1995 by Walker Books Ltd, 87 Vauxhall Walk, London SE11 5HJ

This edition published 2007

2 4 6 8 10 9 7 5 3

©1995 Marcia Williams

The moral rights of the author/illustrator have been asserted.

This book has been typeset in Trump Mediaeval & AT Marigold.

Printed in China

British Library Cataloguing in Publication Data:
a catalogue record for this book is available from the British Library

ISBN 978-1-4063-1137-2

www.walkerbooks.co.uk

The Adventures of
Robin Hood

Retold and Illustrated by

Marcia Williams

WALKER BOOKS
AND SUBSIDIARIES
LONDON · BOSTON · SYDNEY · AUCKLAND

Robin of Locksley
Becomes an Outlaw

Times were hard in medieval England. Good King Richard was away fighting the Crusades, and his evil brother Prince John was gaining wealth and power.

Prince John made the sheriffs and abbots levy taxes and lend money against property. Those who failed to repay a loan lost their homes.

One such was Robin of Locksley who, unable to repay a debt, had been

thrown out of Locksley Hall and was now homeless.

Heartbroken, Robin was wandering through Sherwood Forest when

he came to some foresters out to catch poachers. They taunted Robin, saying he would never dare shoot a deer.

Foolishly, Robin decided to prove them wrong.

Robin's arrow flew straight, killing a fine stag. All the deer belonged to the king and if Robin was caught he could be hanged, which was just what the cruel foresters wanted.

Evading their clutches, Robin started to run, first turning to shoot an arrow into the foresters' midst.

Unintentionally, he struck one dead. As the others paused in horror, they lost sight of Robin.

He ran on, deep into the heart of Sherwood Forest, getting scratched and torn by the thick undergrowth.

Finally he fell exhausted to the ground, tears in his eyes. Robin had never killed a man before.

He swore never to again, and vowed instead to help the poor until King Richard and justice returned to England.

This is precisely what he told a grisly group of outlaws who suddenly burst upon him. They thought it a mad idea.

But they agreed to try it, if Robin could beat them in an archery contest – which, of course, he did.

So the outlaws became the first of Robin's merry men. They nicknamed him Robin Hood and dressed him in Lincoln green.

Robin Gets A Ducking

Robin and his growing band of men built their homes in trees and caves and became skilled in forest lore.

They loved to waylay wealthy travellers, treating them to a forest feast, then making them pay a heavy price.

The travellers left the forest fuller but poorer.

By this means Robin was able to help the truly needy.

If a day passed without a guest he grew restless.

One day, when no wayfarer had been seen for a while,

Robin decided to search further afield, promising his men he would give three blasts on his horn if he ran into trouble. His search eventually brought him to a broad stream spanned by a log.

As he stepped onto the log, a stranger appeared on the other side. The man was seven feet tall and obviously determined to cross first. Robin, equally determined, threatened to shoot him, but resisted as the giant had only a staff for a weapon.

Robin cut himself a staff, then returned to defend "his" log.

For over an hour the battle raged and blow upon blow was struck.

Neither man slipped nor gave an inch to the other.

But at last the giant caught Robin a fierce blow to the legs.

Robin tumbled into the swirling water below.

Laughing at his bad luck, he dragged himself to the bank,

then gave three sharp blasts on his horn as he climbed out.

The two brave men smiled at each other with respect.

They were about to shake hands when a gang of merry men burst from the bushes, ready to defend and protect Robin.

But Robin stayed their hands, for it had been a fair fight and he rather liked the shaggy hulk who had challenged him.

Robin asked his new friend to join the outlaws. He agreed, if Robin could beat him at archery – which, of course, he did.

So John Little, for that was his name, became Robin's right-hand man and friend, and was nicknamed Little John.

Marian Arrives in Sherwood

Later that year, in the house next to Robin's old home, a row took place between his friend Marian Fitzwalter and her father, who wanted her to marry Sir Guy of Gisborne.

Sir Guy was in league with Prince John and his minion, the Sheriff of Nottingham.

The very thought of marrying such a man turned Marian green with horror.

Marian said she would leave home if Sir Guy set one foot inside their house.

So, when Sir Guy came courting through one door,

Marian, disguised as a boy, slipped unseen through another door,

and made her way quickly into the shadows of Sherwood.

At the same time, Robin was out looking for a wealthy guest.

Seeing a likely looking "lad", Robin made him halt and asked him his name. The "lad" was Marian but not recognizing Robin, she refused to answer. Instead, she drew her sword and ordered him to let her pass.

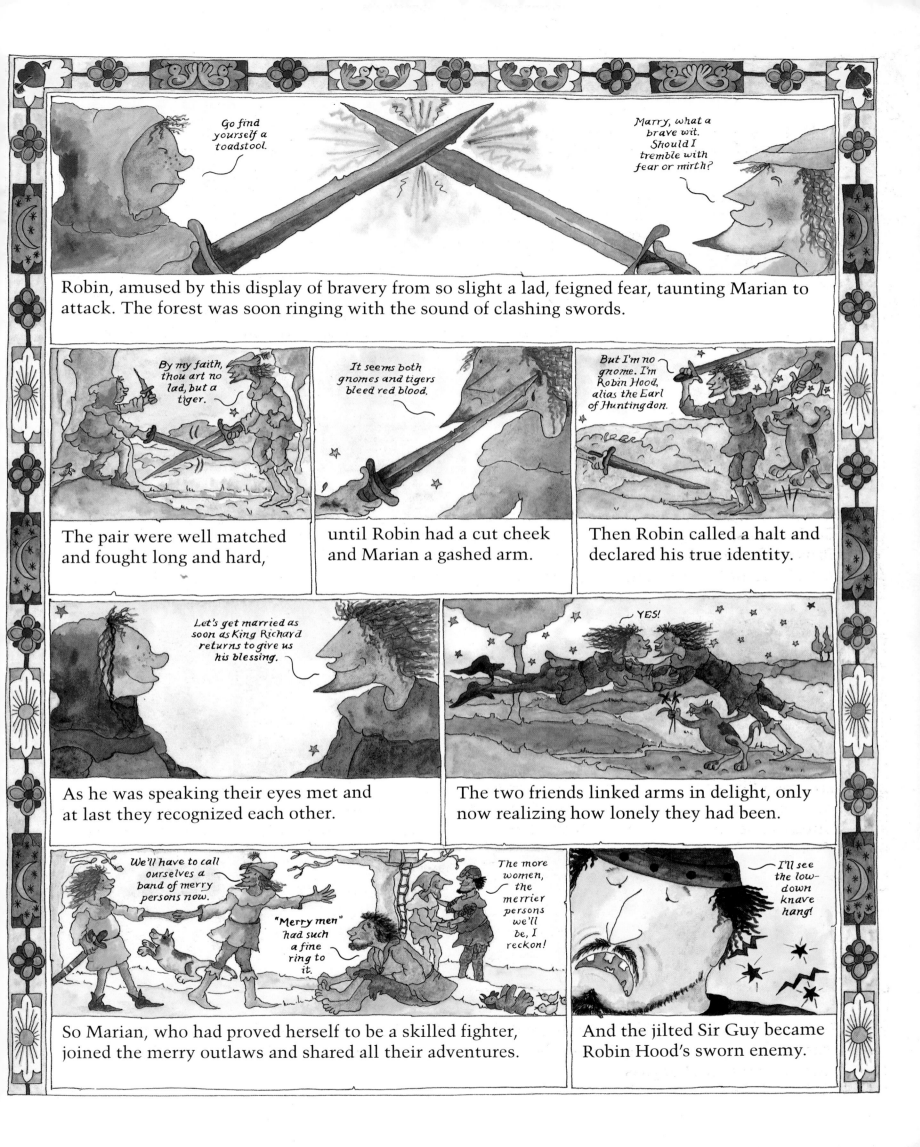

Robin, amused by this display of bravery from so slight a lad, feigned fear, taunting Marian to attack. The forest was soon ringing with the sound of clashing swords.

The pair were well matched and fought long and hard,

until Robin had a cut cheek and Marian a gashed arm.

Then Robin called a halt and declared his true identity.

As he was speaking their eyes met and at last they recognized each other.

The two friends linked arms in delight, only now realizing how lonely they had been.

So Marian, who had proved herself to be a skilled fighter, joined the merry outlaws and shared all their adventures.

And the jilted Sir Guy became Robin Hood's sworn enemy.

The following summer Prince John visited the Sheriff of Nottingham at his castle near Sherwood Forest.

Prince John wanted to know what the sheriff was doing to capture the vexatious outlaw Robin Hood.

The sheriff, who had done nothing about Robin because he feared the outlaws,

tried hard to prove himself loyal to the prince in other ways. The stocks were full,

the hangman's rope frayed with use and the local people taxed into poverty.

Many parents had resorted to begging to feed their children;

some, such as the miller, to poaching the king's deer.

The miller had been unable to pay the burdensome taxes,

so the sheriff burnt down his mill, killing his wife and baby.

The miller had no home and no way to make a living,

so he and his son Much had resorted to shooting deer.

Unluckily, they were caught. Much escaped, but not his father.

The sheriff threatened to blind the miller with hot irons.

Then Prince John rode up, attracted by the miller's screams of terror. The miller begged Prince John for mercy, which the prince promised in return for information about Robin Hood's whereabouts. But no one who knew of Robin's goodness would betray him.

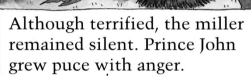

Although terrified, the miller remained silent. Prince John grew puce with anger.

The sheriff, trying to please the prince, ordered his soldier to shoot the miller.

Prince John roared in rage, for he would never learn anything from a dead miller!

As the evil pair rode off, Much crept out of hiding.

Soon, all that could be heard in the forest was his weeping.

And what of his future? Who would feed an extra child?

Then Will Scarlet turned up, carrying food for the poor.

Much ran to Robin's friend Will, begging to be allowed to join the outlaws. Although Much was only twelve years old, Will knew that

Robin would welcome him. This Robin did, and Much proved to be as loyal as his unfortunate father had been.

Friar Tuck

As the days grew shorter, the outlaws spent long hours chatting by the fire. One day Marian told them all about her good friend Friar Tuck and Robin decided he should join them.

Next morning Robin, disguised as a minstrel, set out to find the friar. He thought he was alone,

but Marian and a party of outlaws were close behind.

Robin made his way beside the river to where he had heard Friar Tuck was living as a hermit.

After a time he noticed a fire on the far bank. There was no bridge and the river looked deep and cold. Robin shivered.

Then Robin saw someone he took to be a ferryman. When hailed, the man seemed willing to carry Robin across the river.

He waded over to Robin and then transported the outlaw across, swooshing through the water like a hippopotamus.

As Robin scrambled onto the bank, he felt the prick of steel at his throat. The stranger wanted paying for his services.

When he heard Robin had no purse, the man was on Robin's back in a flash and Robin was forced to return through the icy river.

On reaching the bank, Robin tipped off his fat load and sent the dagger flying with his sword. Now he had the stranger at his mercy.

Robin made the fellow carry him across again.

Once on dry land, the man whirled about, sword drawn: for four hours they battled. For such a fat man, the stranger fought nimbly.

Then Robin got his horn to his lips to summon help.

At the same time his opponent gave a loud whistle.

Seconds later five great hounds bounded to one man's aid and five brave outlaws to the other's. It seemed carnage would result.

But then Marian hugged the stranger, admonishing Robin.

The ferryman was Friar Tuck! And so the fight was soon forgotten over a mug of ale and a warm fire. Robin asked the Friar to join the outlaws and he was delighted, for winter was close at hand and a hermit's life is too lonely for such a jolly friar.

Winter increased Robin's need to raise money for the poor, so he was annoyed when Will Scarlet brought a minstrel called Allan-a-Dale to supper. Allan was indeed unable to pay, his only wealth being half a sixpence, the other half being with his sweetheart.

But seeing tears in the lad's eyes, Robin asked him to tell his tale. It seemed Allan had hoped to marry his love, Ellen, but her avaricious father was forcing her to wed the rich and old Sir Stephen. Robin resolved to help Allan.

Next morning Robin and a band of men, well disguised, set out for the church.

Robin and Friar Tuck entered the church while the others hid outside.

Robin played upon a harp, strumming louder when the bride and groom arrived.

The bishop ordered him to be silent, as the groom was waiting to wed his bride. Robin declared that he saw no groom, only a grandfather. Ellen trembled with misery while her father and Sir Stephen quivered in fury at such insolence.

Undaunted, Robin blew on his horn and the church suddenly filled with outlaws in Lincoln green. "Now Ellen shall marry her own true love," cried Robin, "not this wrinkled walnut." Outraged and outnumbered, Sir Stephen and the bishop fled from the church.

Ellen's disappointed father protested that she could not marry Allan-a-Dale as no banns had been called.

So Friar Tuck mounted the pulpit and called the banns nine times, just in case three was not enough.

Then the Friar wed the happy pair, and even Ellen's father managed a smile after Robin gave him a bag of silver in return for his blessing on the marriage.

Everyone returned to Sherwood for a wedding feast and to listen to Allan's ballads. Ellen and Allan remained friends with the outlaws and their home became a refuge in times of trouble.

Sir Richard of Legh

Another guest who let Robin use his house as a sanctuary was Sir Richard of Legh, whom Little John waylaid on the road to St Mary's Abbey and took home for supper.

Sir Richard was depressed and only picked at his food. He told the gathering a sorry tale of how the abbot had tricked him out of his home by lending him money and then taxing him so that he was unable to repay the debt, which was due at noon the next day.

When Robin told him he had to pay for his meal as well, Sir Richard sighed.

He told Robin his bags were empty; and they were, for Dickon searched them.

So Robin, remembering *his* lost home, gave Sir Richard money to pay his debt.

He also gave him new clothes, asking only that he return in a year to repay the money.

The next day at St Mary's Abbey, the abbot rubbed his hands in glee as noon approached and he could see no sign of Sir Richard of Legh.

Then, to the abbot's horror, at exactly midday, Sir Richard entered.

The frustrated abbot swore he would get Sir Richard's house and land one day.

Exactly one year later, Robin waited for Sir Richard to arrive to repay his debt.

Time passed and the welcome feast began to spoil. Robin sent out a search party.

Unable to find Sir Richard, they detained two monks travelling from the abbey.

Little John scared off their escort, so the monks had to go and eat with Robin.

Robin was delighted when he found the monks were taking £800 to Prince John.

He took the money for the poor and then sent the monks back to St Mary's Abbey.

When Sir Richard finally arrived, Robin let him off repaying the debt.

On hearing about the monks, Sir Richard warned Robin that Prince John was sure to seek revenge. But that didn't stop the outlaws from celebrating. After Robin's kindness to Sir Richard, he and his merry men were always sure to find his house open to them.

The Golden Arrow

COME ONE

COME ALL

Sir Richard was right – Prince John wanted revenge. The prince warned the Sheriff of Nottingham that either he or Robin must go. So the sheriff, Sir Guy of Gisborne and the Abbot of St Mary's hatched a plot. They announced an archery contest to be held at Nottingham. First prize was to be a Golden Arrow. Robin, as his enemies had hoped, could not resist the chance to prove himself the finest archer in England.

The Golden Arrow

ARCHERY CONTEST

BIG PRIZES

HOMELESS

Unaware that it was a trick, Robin disguised the merry band from Sherwood as farmers and himself as a beggar, then travelled to Nottingham to compete in the contest. Flags fluttered and free ale flowed as England's finest archers exercised their skills against each other, until only six were left. The sheriff grew more and more anxious when he failed to see Robin among them. Then only three archers were left and he was convinced that his plan had failed.

The first of the final three to shoot was the sheriff's man, Gilbert. His arrow landed a hair's breadth from the centre of the eye.

The second was Adam O'Dell, a fine marksman. The crowd fell quiet. But his arrow landed just outside the eye.

The sheriff was delighted; he might not have caught Robin but at least his man Gilbert would win the Golden Arrow. Then the third contestant, an unnamed beggar, drew his bow. His arrow flew so true it split Gilbert's in two and embedded itself in the very centre of the eye.

The crowd cheered and clapped, pleased that Gilbert had lost. The sheriff growled furiously. He handed the Golden Arrow to the beggar. Then, thinking he had at least found an archer able to outshoot even Robin Hood, the sheriff offered him a place on his guard – only to be further enraged when his most gracious offer was refused!

Robin was offended that the sheriff should think someone could outshoot him, so he and Little John hatched a plot of their own. That evening, as the sheriff and his henchmen sat bemoaning their failure, an arrow flew through the window, burying itself in the table. Attached to the arrow was this message:

Now heaven bless
thy Grace this day,
Say all in sweet Sherwood.
For thou didst give the prize away
To Merry Robin Hood!

To The Sheriff of N.

Sir Guy of Gisborne

Summer returned to Sherwood. Undaunted by the sheriff's spies, who now continually roamed the forest, Robin and Little John itched for a new adventure.

So, taking separate paths, they set out to see who could find the most excitement.

Robin soon came upon a man dressed entirely in horsehide; even his face was hidden.

When Robin asked the man his name, he drew his sword. It was Sir Guy of Gisborne.

Sir Guy had come to Sherwood determined to slay Robin and claim Maid Marian.

The pair fought savagely, Sir Guy well protected by the hardened horsehide.

But Sir Guy was not as nimble on his feet as the agile Robin Hood.

Finally Robin managed to plunge his sword through a crack in the horsehide and pierce Sir Guy's evil heart.

Robin, realizing he had now broken his vow never to kill, picked up Sir Guy's horn and blew a long, mournful wail.

Meanwhile Little John had found a distraught widow whose two sons were about to be hanged because, driven by hunger, they had killed a royal hind.

Dressed in the dead husband's clothes, Little John went to find the boys.

At the edge of the forest the sheriff was about to hang the two lads.

Unrecognized by anyone, Little John offered his services as hangman.

But when the outlaw put the ropes about the boys' necks he slyly cut their bonds,

urging them to flee into the forest on his command. As he gave the command, however,

and moved to protect them with his bow, the bow snapped in two.

The boys escaped but Little John was caught and his true identity discovered.

Only the sound of Sir Guy's horn saved Little John's life.

The sheriff took it to be a signal that Robin Hood was dead,

and rushed towards the sound to congratulate Sir Guy.

Robin, disguised as Sir Guy, met them on the path.

He indicated that Robin was dead and, as his reward, expressed his wish to kill the sheriff's latest prisoner.

The sheriff unwisely agreed. Seconds later he was being fired upon by the roguish pair of outlaws!

Their laughter rang through the forest as the sheriff and his man fled back to Nottingham Castle.

Robin and Little John then went to invite the grateful boys to join their merry band of forest outlaws.

A Hooded Palmer Visits Sherwood

One autumn, the Bishop of Hereford was travelling through Sherwood Forest accompanied by an unknown, hooded palmer.

Suddenly they were halted by a sword-wielding shepherd and surrounded by outlaws who dropped from the trees.

The shepherd then threw off his disguise, revealing himself to be Robin Hood.

Too scared to protest, the party were led, blindfolded, to partake of a forest feast.

The miserly bishop ate heartily, but refused to pay or to drink a toast to the king.

Angered, Robin made the bishop dance a jig, while his bags were emptied of gold.

As the palmer had no money, Robin suggested he pay for his meal with a game of buffets. The stranger felled all the outlaws. Even Robin was no match for him.

The outlaws then asked the palmer to join them. In reply he doffed his hood,

revealing himself to be King Richard returned from the Crusades. The outlaws knelt, begging the king's pardon. This he freely gave as, led by Robin, they had done much good.

This was the moment that Robin and Marian had longed for – a chance to ask the king's blessing on their marriage. King Richard was delighted to give it, and so, waiting only to put a garland on Marian's head, Friar Tuck wed the joyful couple.

The next day, when all the celebrations were over, the outlaws followed King Richard to Nottingham where, much to everyone's delight, he clamped the wicked sheriff and the miserly Bishop of Hereford into the stocks.

A few of the outlaws then joined King Richard's army, following him back to London, and later to fight in the Crusades.

But most, like Robin and Marian, returned to Sherwood Forest, where they resumed their merry adventures.

So the years slipped happily by. But the outlaws were growing older and one day Marian caught a fever. Tuck nursed her tenderly, but she was weakened by age and died peacefully in her sleep. A special feast was held to honour her, and many people came, as Marian was much loved.

Robin's Last Arrow

Afterwards, Robin tried to keep helping the poor, but he was tired and his body ached.

Little John took Robin to Kirklees Priory to ask the prioress to relieve his pains.

Little John waited while the prioress took Robin in to open a vein, as was the custom.

Afterwards, she said to Robin in icy tones, "Sir Guy of Gisborne was my kinsman." Then Robin heard the key turn in the lock.

The blood flowed from Robin's body, and he knew that he'd been left to die. Summoning the last of his strength, he blew on his horn.

Rushing to Robin's aid, Little John crashed down the door. In one stride he was beside his dearest friend. Robin asked for his bow and, with Little John's help, he fired an arrow through the priory window. Up and over the walls it sped, until it reached the edge of Sherwood Forest. "Bury me wherever the arrow falls," whispered Robin, and closed his eyes.

The outlaws planted an acorn close to where Robin's arrow landed. Over the years it grew into a great oak, under which many generations of merry outlaws have gathered to sing ballads of their great hero Robin Hood and his love, Maid Marian. And so, to this very day, the spirit of Robin Hood lives on in Sherwood Forest.

Marcia Williams

With her distinctive cartoon-strip style, lively text and brilliant wit,
Marcia Williams brings to life some of the world's all-time favourite stories
and some colourful historical characters. Her hilarious retellings and clever
observations will have children laughing out loud and coming back for more!

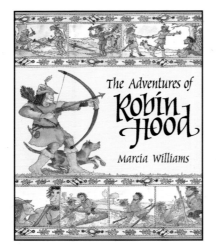

ISBN 978-1-4063-1137-2

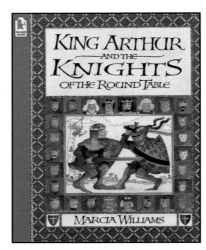

ISBN 978-0-7445-4792-4

ISBN 978-1-4063-0171-7

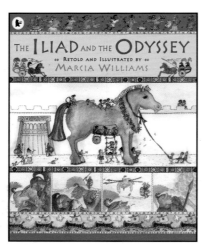

ISBN 978-1-4063-0348-3

ISBN 978-1-4063-0347-6

ISBN 978-1-84428-528-0

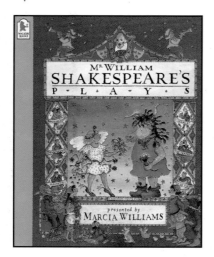

ISBN 978-0-7445-6946-9

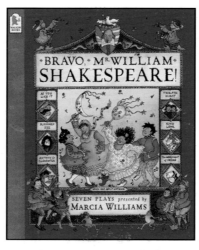

ISBN 978-0-7445-8237-6

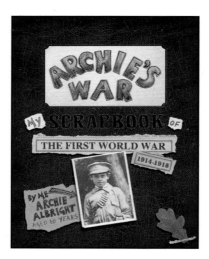

ISBN 978-1-4063-0427-5

Available from all good booksellers